He went to find his brother Lion. He asked Lion what happened at parties.

Lion said there were lots of games to play and food to eat. He said there might be sandwiches, jelly and a birthday cake!

Little Lion liked sandwiches. And he loved cake! He thought parties **might be fun**.

But then Little Lion **began to worry**.
What if he didn't know anyone at the party?
Who would he play with? What **should he do and say** when he got there?
And what if he didn't know how to play the games? Little Lion felt upset. He went to find Mum.

Little Lion told Mum his worries. Mum told Little Lion that she **would stay** at the party with him.

She said Little Lion **already knew** Panda
and he would soon make other friends, too.
Little Lion felt a bit better.

Mum said it was a good idea to **practise** what to do and say at a party. They practised saying hello and giving a present.

They practised saying **please** and **thank you**.
Mum said it was important to remember to say
thank you at the end of a party.

Then Mum said everyone worried sometimes about doing **new things**. She said when she was little, she wanted to join Jungle Club.

But she was worried she wouldn't know anyone. She thought she wouldn't know how to play the games. Mum said she was **too scared** to go into the club. But she took a deep breath and told herself to be brave.

She said everyone at the club made her feel welcome. She made new friends, and they showed her how to play the games. It was fun!

Little Lion had a think. He said he could **be brave**, too. Mum said that was a **good idea**.

Soon it was the day of Panda's party.

Little Lion wrapped Panda's present carefully.

He **wrote her name** carefully on the label.

Then Mum took him to Panda's house. Little Lion was scared. But he remembered what Mum said. He took a **deep breath**. He told himself to **be brave**. Little Lion knocked on the door.

He said hello to Panda and gave her the present.
Panda was very pleased.

Everyone made Little Lion feel welcome. He made lots of friends. He ate lots of sandwiches … and jelly … and birthday cake! It was all **delicious**.

23

Then it was time for party games. Little Lion was worried. He didn't know **how to play them**. But he wanted to join in. He took a deep breath. He told himself to be brave. Everyone **showed him what to do**.

Soon Little Lion knew how to play all the games. He even won a prize for Sleeping Lions. Everyone said he was the best sleeping lion of all!

Then it was time to go home. Little Lion remembered to thank Panda and Panda's mum for inviting him. He told Mum that parties were **brilliant fun**, and he couldn't wait to go to another one!

# A note about sharing this book

The *Experiences Matter* series has been developed to provide a starting point for further discussion on how children might deal with new experiences. It provides opportunities to explore ways of developing coping strategies as they face new challenges.

The series is set in the jungle with animal characters reflecting typical behaviour traits and attitudes often seen in young children.

### *Little Lion Goes to a Party*

This story looks at the worries a child might have when going to a party for the first time. It highlights the most typical concerns and suggests strategies for dealing with them, especially practising party protocol before the event itself to give the child confidence.

### How to use the book

The book is designed for adults to share with either an individual child, or a group of children, and as a starting point for discussion.

The book also provides visual support and repeated words and phrases to build reading confidence.

### Before reading the story

Choose a time to read when you and the children are relaxed and have time to share the story.

Spend time looking at the illustrations and talk about what the book might be about before reading it together.

Encourage children to employ a phonics-first approach to tackling new words by sounding the words out.

28

**After reading, talk about the book with the children:**

- Ask the children why Little Lion was anxious about going to a party for the first time. Have any of the children had similar worries? Do they feel more reassured if a parent or carer goes with them?

- Talk about the idea of practising what to say and do at a party. Do the children's parents or carers remind them to say please and thank you, and especially to thank the host at the end of the party?

- Why was Little Lion concerned about party games? Have the children had similar concerns when a game that is new to them has been played? How did they manage? Did others take time to explain how to play the game? Remind the children to be aware of others at a party who may need some extra help.

Remind the children to listen carefully while others speak and to wait for their turn.

- Divide the children into small groups. Choose a child to be the party giver and the others to be the guests. Ask the host to act out how they would greet their guests and look after them. Ask the others in each group to be the guests and to act out how they would respond.

- At the end of the session, choose groups to show their responses to the others.

*For Isabelle, William A, William G, George, Max, Emily,*
*Leo, Caspar, Felix, Tabitha, Phoebe, Harry and Libby –S.G.*

Franklin Watts
First published in 2023 by
Hodder & Stoughton

Text © Hodder & Stoughton Limited, 2023
Illustrations © Trevor Dunton, 2023

The right of Trevor Dunton to be identified as the illustrator
of this Work has been asserted in accordance with the
Copyright, Designs and Patents Act, 1988.

Editor: Jackie Hamley
Designer: Cathryn Gilbert

A CIP catalogue record for this book is available
from the British Library.

ISBN 978 1 4451 8208 7 (hardback)
ISBN 978 1 4451 8209 4 (paperback)
ISBN 978 1 4451 8871 3 (ebook)

Printed in China

Franklin Watts
An imprint of
Hachette Children's Books,
Part of Hodder & Stoughton
Carmelite House
50 Victoria Embankment
London EC4Y 0DZ

An Hachette UK company
www.hachettechildrens.co.uk